The Grumpy Little Girls and the Wobbly Sleepover

FIZ

REAL NAME: Felicity.
Yurgh!

BESTEST THING: Bouncing on
my trampoline

WANTS V V V V MUCH:
To learn to do a proper
cartwheel

HATES: Playing quietly indoors

GETS GRUMPY: When my big
brothers sit on me...

Maisie

BESTEST FRIEND: Lulu

PETS: Only the Blob –
(my baby brother!)

FAVOURITE GAME:
Let's Pretend!

YUMMIEST FOOD: Slimy
worms (Spaghetti, silly!)

SCARIEST SCARY THING:
Spiders. Eeeek!

GETS GRUMPY:
When Lulu won't play
Let's Pretend....

Ruby

LOVES: Horse riding and karate lessons

HATES: Piano lessons. Snore!

WANTS V V V V MUCH: A pony and pierced ears. (But mum says I've got to wait till I'm 12!)

FAVOURITE COLOUR: Pink, pink, pink!

GETS GRUMPY: When Maisie and Lulu and Fiz won't do what I tell them...

favourite cat

LULU

BESTEST FRIEND: Maisie. (Or Warren, my woodlouse.)

PETS: 3 cats, 12 fish, 2 guinea pigs, 4 Giant Amazonian snails, 1 rabbit, 1 rat, 1 woodlouse

WANTS V V V MUCH: A ferret!

YUKKIEST FOOD: Meat

GETS GRUMPY: When mum makes me clean out my pets' cages...

First published in Great Britain by HarperCollins*Publishers* Ltd in 2000

1 3 5 7 9 10 8 6 4 2

ISBN: 0 00 664709 X

Concept copyright © Arroyo Projects 2000

Text and characters copyright © Lindsay Camp 2000

Illustrations copyright © Daniel Postgate 2000

The author and illustrator assert the moral right to be identified
as the author and illustrator of the work.

The HarperCollins website address is:
www.**fire**and**water**.com

Printed and bound in Singapore.

The Grumpy Little Girls and the Wobbly Sleepover

Lindsay Camp and Daniel Postgate

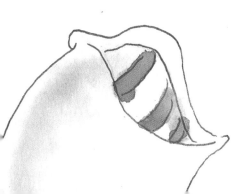

Collins

An imprint of HarperCollins Publishers

Lulu was staying the night at Maisie's.

They lived next door to each other and had *been* best friends since they were *babies*, so they often stayed over with each other.

Lulu had brought Alvin with her.

After their bath, they played Circus Ladies, and taught Alvin to do all kinds of tricks.

At bedtime, when Maisie's mum came up to say goodnight, the girls were whispering together.

"What is it?" she asked. "What are you two planning now?"

"We were wondering... " said Lulu, a bit shyly.

" ...if we could have a sleepover?" finished Maisie.

"Isn't this a sleepover?" asked Maisie's mum.

"No, silly," said Maisie. "A proper real one – with popcorn, and videos and lots of people."

"Hm," said Maisie's mum doubtfully. "I'm not sure. I'll have to talk to dad about it."

Maisie was rather grumpy after her mum went downstairs,
because "talking to dad" nearly always meant no.

"Never mind," said Lulu. "We'll ask my mum and dad in the morning."

So they did.

But Lulu's mum and dad said no straight away.

"Maybe one day," said Lulu's mum.

"Nobody would get a wink of sleep," said Lulu's dad.

"It's not fair!" complained Lulu and Maisie together, very grumpily indeed.

But just then, something happened that made Lulu cheer up. Something inside her mouth. Wriggling her tongue around, she noticed something – well, loose.

"Hey," she shouted. "I've got a wobbly tooth!" She poked it with her finger. There was no doubt about it, it was her very first wobbly tooth.

"Come and see," she said to Maisie.
"You can wobble it if you like."
But Maisie didn't want to.

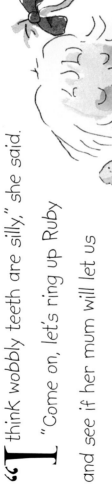

"I think wobbly teeth are silly," she said.

"Come on, let's ring up Ruby and see if her mum will let us have a sleepover."

Ruby was very excited when she answered the phone.

"You'll never guess what!" she said. "I've got a wobbly tooth!"

"So have I!" said Lulu.

"Ask her about the sleepover," hissed Maisie, crossly.

Ruby's mum said no, too.

But on Monday at school, when Lulu and Ruby had shown each other their wobbly teeth, they told Fiz about the sleepover. And she said they could definitely have one at her house.

Fiz had three very big brothers, and her house was always full of teenagers in sleeping bags. So she was sure her mum and dad wouldn't mind at all.

And she was right. They said it would be absolutely fine, and that they could have the sleepover next Saturday night.

The girls were very excited.

"I bet my wobbly tooth will have fallen out by then," said Lulu.

"I bet mine will come out before yours," said Ruby.

"Hey," said Maisie, with her finger in her mouth. "I think one of my teeth is just a tiny bit wobbly...."

After that, the Great Wobbly Tooth Race began. Whenever Lulu, Ruby or Maisie didn't have anything else to do with their fingers, they wobbled furiously.

Only Fiz didn't join in. She was too busy learning to skip backwards.

At last, the day of the sleepover arrived. In the car on the way to Fiz's house, Lulu and Maisie were still wobbling away.

"I bet Ruby's tooth has come out," said Lulu. "She said she was going to tie a piece of string round it, and then tie the string to a door handle, and slam the door."

"That's cheating!" said Maisie.

But when they arrived, they found Ruby's tooth still hanging on to Ruby's gum. Soon, they all forgot about their teeth and started to enjoy their sleepover.

Ruby

LOVES: Horse riding and karate lessons

HATES: Piano lessons. Snore!

WANTS V V V V MUCH: A pony and pierced ears. (But mum says I've got to wait till I'm 12!)

FAVOURITE COLOUR: Pink, pink, pink!

GETS GRUMPY: When Maisie and Lulu and Fiz won't do what I tell them...

favourite cat

LULU

BESTEST FRIEND: Maisie. (Or Warren, my woodlouse.)

PETS: 3 cats, 12 fish, 2 guinea pigs, 4 Giant Amazonian snails, 1 rabbit, 1 rat, 1 woodlouse

WANTS V V V MUCH: A ferret!

YUKKIEST FOOD: Meat

GETS GRUMPY: When mum makes me clean out my pets' cages...

Have you read all the stories about us?

The Grumpy Little Girls and the Princess Party
ISBN 0 00 664708 1

The Grumpy Little Girls and the Wobbly Sleepover
ISBN 0 00 664709 X

The Grumpy Little Girls and the Bouncy Ferret
ISBN 0 00 664770 7

The Grumpy Little Girls and the Naughty Little Boy
ISBN 0 00 664769 3